W9-DJD-118

The Horse That Looked Different

by Stacy Einfalt

Text and Illustrations Copyright©
2014 By Stacy Einfalt

I would like to dedicate this story to my baby girl,
my heart, and my best friend; to my horse Gotcha.
3/24/1984-1/12/2012

Out in the middle of the countryside amongst rolling hills of planted farmland, Mr. and Mrs. Brown along with their two daughters live on a small farm, Happy Acres.

2

3

Living with them at Happy Acres are their three chestnut colored quarter horses Max, Milo, and Monty and their two dogs Ginger and Cocoa.

Mr. and Mrs. Brown and their older daughter Carly, enjoy taking their horses on trail rides. Their younger daughter Lexi usually follows along with Ginger and Cocoa.

Lexi has been taking riding lessons for the past few years and her parents feel she is ready to have a horse of her own. That way she would be able to join them when they go for trail rides.

The family began searching near and far in efforts to find a horse for Lexi.

Many days went by until they finally found the
perfect match for her.

He was a ten-year-old Appaloosa gelding. What Mr. and Mrs. Brown liked most about him was his quiet, gentle manner. Lexi's sister loved his striped feet. Lexi liked the coat of white hair that covered his rump and white spots that sprinkled his black coat. She thought they looked like a blanket of stars in the night sky.

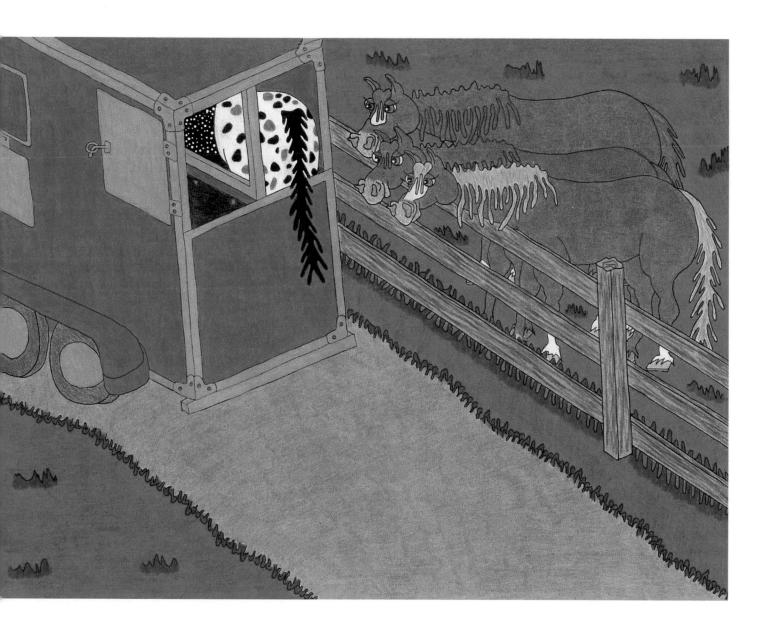

Before they could get him home, Lexi decided on a name for him. She was going to call him Starlit. When they pulled into the driveway back home at Happy Acres, Max, Milo, and Monty came running up to the pasture fence. Their eyes wide open with excitement waiting to see what the new horse looked like.

When Starlit came off of the trailer the other horses gave out a big snort and took a few steps backward. They looked at one another, confused. They had never seen a horse that looked like that.

Lexi's dad walked Starlit into the pasture. The other horses began prancing around with their tails in the air.

When he took off Starlit's halter he trotted across the pasture to meet the other horses. As he got closer to them they began pinning their ears back and flaring their nostrils.

Then suddenly they charged him, chasing him away. Starlit then knew that the other horses did not want him to be a part of their small herd. It made Lexi feel sad, "I don't think they like him because he looks different." Her mother tried comforting her by saying, "Don't worry they will be friends before we know it."

A few days went by but Max, Milo, and Monty still would not allow Starlit to graze with them. Each time he would try, they would chase him away. Starlit had to graze all by himself on the other end of the pasture.

He was feeling sad and lonely. He began to wish he didn't have his wild spotted coat and striped feet. He wished he could look like the others, maybe then they would accept him.

Lexi was watching how the other horses still were not allowing Starlit to become a part of their group. She felt badly for him having to be off by himself, away from the others. She decided to go out and sit with Starlit to keep him company while grazing. Once she sat down, Starlit walked over and gently rubbed his nose on her cheek, letting her know he was happy she was there.

After sitting and watching him for a while Lexi could hear her mother calling her to come in for dinner. She jumped up, gave Starlit a kiss, and took off across the pasture.

When she got to the pasture gate she opened it and ran up
towards the house, forgetting to close the gate behind her.

It only took a few moments for Max, Milo, and Monty to notice that the pasture gate was open. They knew this was their chance to go on a wild adventure, so they took off galloping through the open gate. Even though Starlit knew the others wouldn't want him to come along, he decided to follow them anyway.

The four horses ran across their property until they reached
the neighbor farmer Joe's cornfield.

Without a second thought, they ran through the cornfield
leaving a path of trampled corn stalks behind them.

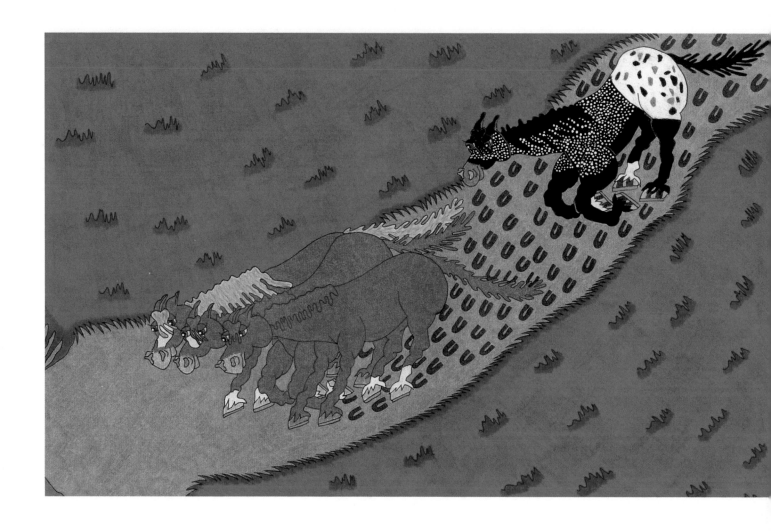

They reached the edge of the cornfield and ran down a hill where
they came upon a flowing stream.

Max, Milo, and Monty jumped down into the
water and began stomping their feet, splashing
themselves, and each other to cool off.

Starlit hesitated and stood up on the bank watching the others. That's when they realized Starlit was following them on their adventure. Once again they pinned their ears and glared their eyes at Starlit, letting him know they didn't want him along with them.

They then turned, ran up the other side of the bank and into the woods. Starlit, even though not invited, crossed the stream and continued to follow the others down the path through the woods.

They reached the edge of the woods that opened up into a clearing
filled with lush, green grass.

Max, Milo, and Monty were hungry from their long journey.
They walked out into the clearing and began munching on grass.
Starlit tried walking over and joining them, but again
they chased him away.

Starlit went off to another area in the clearing and grazed by
himself. Evening was setting in, and the sun was going down.

The horses were growing worried, realizing they were far from home and not sure how to get back.

Back home at Happy Acres, the Brown's finished dinner and set out towards the barn to bring the horses in from the pasture and put them in their stalls for the evening.

They reached the pasture and saw that the gate was open and there were no horses. Lexi realized she forgot to shut the gate earlier. She felt horrible. "It's my fault!" Lexi exclaimed. "What are we going to do Mommy?"
"Well, we need to go look for them honey," her mother said.

The family began looking for clues to help them figure out which direction the horses went. Suddenly Carly yelled out, "Over here! There are hoof prints across the back yard that lead up to farmer Joe's cornfield!"

They reached the cornfield and could see the path of corn
stalks that had been trampled.

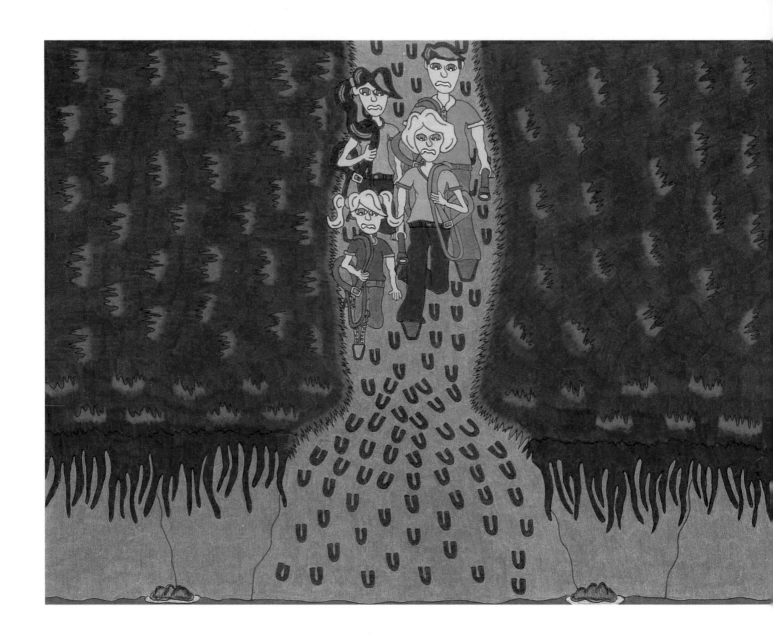

They followed the path of trampled corn until they got to the hill.
It was growing darker by the minute, Lexi's mom and dad turned
on their flashlights.

When they arrived at the stream they could see hoof
prints on either side of the bank by the stream.

They crossed the stream and found the
path that goes through the woods.

Following the path, the family made it through the woods and out into the clearing. They began scanning their eyes across the open area hoping they would find them. Suddenly Lexi saw what looked to be a big cluster of stars twinkling against the night sky.

She shouted out with excitement, "Starlit, is that you?"
They could hear a high pitched whinny followed
by a herd of galloping feet coming towards them.

The family along with the horses were so relieved. Max, Milo, and Monty realized that if it weren't for Starlit's spots shining in the moonlight, they might not have been found.

The Brown's led the horses back to Happy Acres and
put them into their stalls for the evening, so they
could rest up from their wild adventure.

When morning came the family went out and put the
horses into their pastures, then stood by the fence
and watched them interact with each other.

Max, Milo, and Monty walked up to Starlit and began nuzzling on him. They were letting Starlit know they were finally accepting him into their small herd, even though he looked different from them. They could now appreciate his wild spotted coat and striped feet. They realized that they too had special markings that made them unique.

Lexi said, "Look, I think they have finally become friends!"
From that day on the four horses were best buddies. They enjoyed
running, playing, and grazing with one another in the pasture.

73124145R00029

Made in the
USA
Middletown, DE